CW00370161

WINDHORSE

Also by John Killick

Would You Please Give Me Back My Personality?
(University of Stirling)

Ed. The Times of Our Lives
(Westminster Health Care)

Ed. Between the Lines, Between the Bars
(Other Voices)

John Killick

WINDHORSE

To Jackie and Paul
With Best Wishes
(and admiration)
John Killick

Rockingham Press

Published by
The Rockingham Press
11 Musley Lane,
Ware, Herts
SG12 7EN

British Library Cataloguing-in-Publication Data

A catalogue record for this book
is available from the British Library

ISBN 1 873468 42 3

Printed in Great Britain
by Bemrose Shafron (Printers) Ltd,
Chester

Printed on Recycled Paper

This book is for
Carole, Angus, Emma and Jessica

Acknowledgements

Acknowledgements are due to the following magazines and books where some of these poems first appeared:

Lines Review, The London Magazine, The North, Northlight, Pennine Platform, The Pennine Poets Anthologies 1986 and 1991, The Poetry Business Anthology 1990, Poetry SouthEast 3, The Scottish Review, Sheaf, Span, Tandem, The Times Literary Supplement, The Wide Skirt, the pamphlets *Continuous Creation* (1979), *A Pennine Chain* (1983), *Things Being Various* (1987) and *Singular Persons* (1988), and the anthology *The Land Out There* (Aberdeen University Press, 1991)

The author is very grateful to Mimi Khalvati, Myra Schneider and Peter Sansom for advice on individual poems.

Notes

A Windhorse is a rope tied with pieces of coloured cloth, which Tibetan nomads use as a divining instrument to guide their wanderings.

'My Head is for the Heights' is a variation on a line by Sorley Maclean.

'Anna, With Mushrooms' is Anna Adams.

'Sketches of Lowry' draws upon an Interview with Mervyn Levy.

'Janacek' and 'The Composer and the Birds' include material from the composer's journalism.

'Three From Inside' are poems from a Prison Sequence.

'The Gooseberry Game' is based on an article by Alan Garner.

Contents

Windhorse	11
Travelling	12
Survivor	13
My Head is for the Heights	14
Curlew	15
Incongruity	16
Kingcombe	17
Berrying	18
Nightlights	19
Stone in the Stream	20
Lewisian Gneiss Outcrops	21
The Sound of Harris	22
Sea Farmer	23
Return of the Native	24
Barra Burial Ground	25
Metaphor For Mairi	26
Anna, With Mushrooms	27
Sketches of Lowry	28
Buffet	32
The Homer's Odyssey	34
Doo-Love	36
Elegy for an Attercliffe Barber	37
Painting the Light	38
Goodbye My Loves	40
Chiaroscuro	41
Monsoon	43
Nomads	44
In Nebraska, Dakota & Beyond ...	45
Harlem Airshaft	46
Going to Mmbatho	47
Under the Wall	50
Three From Inside	51
Hit or Miss	54
In the Day-Centre	55
Janacek	56

Nuns With Chamber Orchestra 57
Movements 58
The Gooseberry Game 60
The Composer and the Birds 62
In the Garden 63
Garden of Love 64
Dream-Sequence 65
Night Train 67
The Snowman 68
Divining 69
Triptych 70
Losing Win 72
Hospice Voices 74
Last Photograph of the Mother-in-law 76
After Image 77
Lines on Lines 78

WINDHORSE

Flags of all the nations
are only worth the rags
they can be torn into.

I follow the way they blow
over rivers and mountains
crossing invisible frontiers.

Every 'highway to success',
every 'road less travelled by',
is an irrelevancy.

Each morning is a departure
on a course without decision.

Each evening an arrival
at a place without destination.

I write down words confident
that the wind will scatter them.

TRAVELLING

They gave up everything,
as I wanted to once,
to cultivate some warm
patch of West Wales
and contemplate sun-
flowers they have grown
higher than themselves.

I could do it now,
probably better than then,
but I'm past the wanting
the mind turning
in upon itself —
the vegetal response
to the human possible.

As you descend the slope
the horizon clamps down,
hillsides funnel you in.
But keep on walking
as if all depends upon
the view from the watershed
of the next valley but one.

SURVIVOR

That day Pearson Dalton awoke
to the same dawn wilderness,
scene of a life-time's travail
(sixteen-hundred-feet up in untracked
fell country at the back of Skiddaw),
shrugged into his clothes and
shifted his seventy-five-year carcass
of bones from the window and out
to where the farmer's jeep awaited
the sum of his familiars (pots, pans,
oil-lamp, bedding, battered radio-set,
thirteen-year-old cat, and nanny-goat
rumoured at twenty-two), saw them go,
and tidied and locked for the last time
this tilted shooting-box he had first come to
in '22 on a month's trial, and stuck,
four mountain miles from the human,
in thrall to the seasons and the insistent
call of his flock, then down the slope
(five dogs at heel), round Great Calva
to his sister's at Caldbeck — into the fold.

MY HEAD IS FOR THE HEIGHTS

My head is for the heights:
to stand dizzying on a ridge
which before me rises higher.
Only the way is rough, and barred
by huge boulders, and marred
by cliff-falls into corries
of dark dimensionless desolation.
I climb, stumble and fall —
onto a hairsbreadth ledge.
I'm only just hanging on.
My feet can't feel the ground.
No use. It's all beyond me.
Even at this level I'm unable
to lower a rope to my heart.

CURLEW

Where the bald path strikes across the moor,
winds stunt the bushes, and scour
the few trees almost to extinction,
and the persistent rain serves only
the peat-bogs' unslakeable thirst —

these are haunting grounds of the curlew:
almost an exhalation of the earth,
a whistling in the light, then a recurrent
nocturnal call, embodiment
of landscape giving up its ghost.

INCONGRUITY

It was a common-or-field manure heap,
as we could smell from a distance,
but when we got close it glistened
with the interweavings of a thousand webs;
a network of spiders' traps covered the surface,
lifting in the wind, fraying at gusts.
We marvelled awhile at such a congress
(incongruous bridal: dung clothed in the ethereal),
and left there, unlikely in its landscape,
a midden with a halo in the sun.

KINGCOMBE

Yonder Cowleaze, Neals Wood, Mowlands Common —
the old doles are still visible
as banks and hedgerows, fossilized for posterity.

From a distance fields ripple like beasts' flanks
but come into close focus as
phalanxes of mauve and olive seedheads.

Swallows hover and spurt overhead.
Marbled whites sit sunning themselves.
Grasshoppers give voice to the quivering air.

Elsewhere they have pulled the grass
out from under our feet
but in Kingcombe it still stands tall —

the land Arthur Walbridge loved
and left inviolate; profligate
small harvest; last lost world.

BERRYING

After long drought,
uncommon sun,
berries plentiful
are large, lustrous,

great pendulous
globes of moisture
as if to slake
thirst of the earth

tremulous to touch
and sensual
as nipples they
draw me down —

can't get enough —
for hours after
berries fruiting
and filling my mind.

NIGHTLIGHTS

1

Your curve is an ache
that has not found a body,
half-moon in the sky.

2

Snow-flakes are falling
all night in through the window
with a little hiss
giving up their crystal ghosts
white upon black on the sill.

3

The candle's remains:
a midget's causeway of grease
in the morning light.

STONE IN THE STREAM

In the lucent light
the stream ripples,
eddies around a stone.
The current winnows
the sun, fronds waver,
tadpoles and minnows
in sudden spurts
change direction —
life teems about it
but the stone stands
clear of imprecision.

Weed surrounds the stone
but the stone sustains.
It is not shaken,
though all about it
are darting differences.
No stone in isolation
has such stability,
and only by immersion
can strong identity
cohere about a core.

LEWISIAN GNEISS OUTCROPS

A landscape of lumps of stone.
Yes, I know there's grass
and a few scrubby trees
but the rock is everywhere,
poking its bones out at all angles,
and man squats uncomfortably between.

It's called 'close to Nature'
or 'the bare necessities'
this continually being nudged to awareness
of where we come in the end.

Yet out of this place have grown
the tongue's impassioned flowering,
grace-notes of elation.

THE SOUND OF HARRIS

What is that sound upon the air, a faint
susurration of the marram-grass fronds?
Rather a coronach that fills with dread,
drawn as it were from out the landscape's heart,
a long low keening with the measured tread
of generations of the island dead.

Or that year's final crop of families
straggling the strand with their belongings
(creels, spades and bibles) freeing from the throat
the communal wail of the dispossessed,
which, as the cortege enters in the boat,
fails to a single bagpipe's reedy note.

Drowned now beneath the waves' absolving sound
'husinish, husinish' upon the sand.

SEA FARMER

Our forebears had never entered a boat
before the day they were chased out of Uist.
Their children sat down in the stern
because it happened to be first along the quay
and they thought that it would get there before.

Now we have become skilled in the ways
of husbandry of the sea. All our talk
is of seines and shoals, of creels, crans and curers,
and we hearken to the Word of the force forecasts.
Our womenfolk, who once had been
oblivious even of the gulls' girning,
now spend long hours scanning the sea-murk,
have learned the rituals of headland mourning.
Our own bairns hold wetted fingers aloft
to catch the wind's alarms. All are on ocean alert.

Truly the taste in our mouths is salt:
the land we tilled before could not support us,
and now we walk the shifting waves unsteadily.
Wherever we look, the furrows of our wake
close over as if we had never ploughed there.

RETURN OF THE NATIVE

In exile, he took the colours from the cloth.
Now he would give them back to the landscape where
they belonged:
reddy-browns to the sun-scorched lichens,
purple and green to the heather-tops,
obsidian to the outcrops of rocks,
white to the sands and grey to the shallows,
cool blues into the translucency of the air.
Thus having unburdened himself of his memories
he had no need of the tweeds.

BARRA BURIAL-GROUND

After life-times of the staggers,
bracing against the sliding slabs
and tossed at last into the troughs,
these men should surely have won home
to haven of some inland strath,

not this shaken funeral-ship
as if towed behind the island,
tangled with weed, crusted with salt,
its freight under perpetual
threat from breakers marbled with foam:

the seafarers' cemetery,
a place never outwith the sound
of waves drowning again the drowned.

METAPHOR FOR MAIRI

Some see our island as the world's end
(or beginning) of geological time,
and it is true that mica-sparkled gneiss,
barren, domed and ridged, with the imprint
of glacial striae or scratchings, gives the eye
no relief from abrasive surfaces,
and if this were all there is
might justify such a calling.

But for a contrast (could there be one more extreme!)
there is the machair: where sand forms the base,
siliceous, calcareous, and supports marram,
which soaks up the water yet imparts stability,
a dense network anchored in perpetuity.
Sea-sedge forms a green coverlet
upon which floats a floral
pattern of vetch, gentian and trefoil.

Her beauty partakes of this quality
of astonishment: rich, rooted, plebeian.

ANNA, WITH MUSHROOMS

I went to see her, where
foliage burgeoned about her door,
Penyghent loured in the background,
ceramic creatures and poems
crowded round her desk. I found
her fragile, defensive,
wearing the hurt puzzlement
of the too-long ignored.

Back home, I walk tracks
of my moist valley.
Everywhere fungal fruiting
bodies, forest show-offs,
blurting their spores —
many ugly milk-caps
have had their heads knocked off.

But part the grasses and find
seasonal signs of symbiosis
ever-present underneath —
the amonitas holding their ground.

SKETCHES OF LOWRY

1

Hey, hey. I go
on doing them, don't I?
Do you think so?
Do you really?
Do you really like it?
Oh I am pleased,
that's very nice.
You think I have?
Do you? You know,
I think I like it,
I think I do,
I don't think I'll do
any more to it,
no, I don't think I shall.
Oh well,
that's very nice,
I am pleased.

2

Do you like that
gentleman?   He was at
a match between
Manchester City and
Sheffield United.
He was very upset
about the standard of play.
He threw down his pork-pie
and walked off in high dudgeon.
Note
the smallness
of the ears.

3

I asked her.
I said, will you sit
for me for half-an-hour,
and she said she would,
but after a bit
I said, I don't know
how to start you —
you bother me
sat there!
But she was very good,
she said oh,
you'll be alright.

I had a spasm
of painting her.
That's her, oh yes,
it's very like her,
I think I've got
everything in. She made me
listen to Bellini.
I thought he was harmless,
but now I particularly
like him,
I very *particularly*
like Bellini.

4

You do?
You remember
that lady pushing the pram?
Well I saw her,
I saw her in Winchester.

Oh the language,
the language was appalling,
I turned pale.
In Winchester
of all places, sir!

I don't like
to think about it!

5

Look — in here!
There's father, oh
fifty years ago
I did poor father,
how they carried on,
they said
it was wicked!
Well I didn't do
what I might have done
with father, but I did
what I wanted.

6

I was very bothered
about a car in 1924.
Mother, I said
if you buy a car
I'll drive you out.
But she didn't take
to the idea, oh no,
not at all. "We'll wait
till your father comes in."

When father came home
he just said
three words:
“The man’s mad!”
It bothered me
at the time, but I
don’t think I would
have made a driver,
no I
don’t think I should.

7

I’ve been meaning to
move from here for oh
I don’t know
how many years,
but I don’t know
where to go,
I don’t know
where I’d *like* to go.
I used to look at maps
when I was a young man
going on my holidays,
and I couldn’t see
anywhere I wanted to go.
In fact,
if I looked at the map
long enough, I’d start
disliking everywhere
very violently indeed!

BUFFET

1

The buffet is full of travellers,
taxi-drivers, and those going nowhere.

Suddenly a youth with staring hair
and eyes, oil-stained sweater
and frayed jeans, lurches to the counter,
grabs a fistful of tissues
and collapses by the jukebox,
his whole frame racked with sobs.

"Mam, mam" — a child pulls at her coat.
"Wotsit naw? Warrive yer seen?
Yer not ter bovver wiv that boo bloody hoo!"

Cigarette-smoke rises to the strip-lights.
Discs spin on the fruit-machine:
coins spill out as someone wins.

2

"Nobbut's sayin' nowt about owt in 'ere.
That's what let 'em in int' first place.
Germans — the sign they're tekkin ower
is where yer see black'n-white buildins."
The small silver-haired lady
takes her handbag to the counter,
pays for her fish-and-chips.
Sits. Eats. Nobbut's sayin' nowt.

Then she starts again. "They're organisin'
from't shipyard i' Barrow-in't-Furness.

One mornin' yer won't wekkup,
I'se warnin' yer. An' 'ter Queen's
i' league wi'em. She 'as
Germans wi' machine-guns
on sentry-duty outside t'Palace.
But mostly their approach is insiderus —
wipin' us out wi' cancer 'n diabetes
in't Methodist Church 'n St Chad's.

Ay, Officer, is there onniethin' wrong?
I saw someone'd nicked t'vinegar.
I'll go wi' yer onny road if yer
promise not t' tek me inside
one o' them black'n-white buildins."

Silence. Everyone knows it happened.
But nobbut's sayin' nowt about it.

3

The old grow older here,
trivially drivelling,
trousers at half-mast,
they grub in ashtrays
or ogle yuppies for cash.

Here's one can't stay still,
emptying dregs from paper-cups
down his scrawny throat,
endlessly trundling a circular
track round the tables.

Now he pauses at the door
to the platform watching Inter-
Citys swish past: a world
and a few feet away —
he's buffet-bound for ever.

THE HOMER'S ODYSSEY

It were Leakey the Dealer
that gave me the blue cock,
and 'e were a laggard.
I thought, I'll send 'im on
'is own to't South of France:
either I'll lose 'im
or I'll mek 'im come.

It would've been around
'alf-five when they was tossed.
They should've been back
'ome by 'alf-four.
'Alf-four I ring Club up —
they'd not 'eard nowt.
'Alf-five — not a sign.
'Alf-six, then 'alf-seven —
I said, I've lost 'im!
Then quarter-to-ten — Bang!
I let rip: "Where the bloody
'ell've you been?"

When all came to all,
though, 'e were the only
bird to return to Lancashire.
There were misery in't lofts
that night — five 'undred birds lost!

I couldn't weigh it up,
why 'e weren't chosen.
Then one day flyin' round
'e went 'n missed 't wire.
I thought, ay, that's it,
it's 'is bloody eyes.

I tried 'im out after —
clear case o' short sight.

'Ow 'e were thinkin' was:
Oh, I've seen that steeple,
I've passed that chimbley —
and that's 'ow a 'alf-blind
bird went 'n got 'isself 'ome.

As for t'other buggers,
they all went t'other road!

DOO-LOVE

If the sun promises to shine
two men from Carntyne,
Hammy Hamilton and Chick Caven,
(the uncrowned king of doo-men)
leg it to the lofts:

pitch-black like pill-boxes,
protected by padlocks
and steel bolts. Imprisoned within —
the doos men have died for.
"It's Fort Knox wi' feathers."

They stop there for a blether,
a bit of banter or
to slag each other off:
"That loft of yours is boggin
and in need of a good clean."

"You have to doll your doo up.
Some guys use hair-dyes
painted on wi' a wee brush.
Then keep their peroxide blondes
horny or on the ramp."

Hammy speaks an Esperanto
to his doo, wooing her with words.
Chick opens his huge hands,
caresses the fragile span,
then nestles her next to his chest.

When they look out over the
scrubby waste-tips, raw
schemes, draggled plots,
all they see is sheer white,
all they feel is soft down.

ELEGY FOR AN ATTERCLIFFE BARBER

He rides a unicycle
fixed by an iron bar
pivoting on the pedestal
of his barber's chair.

Turning about 180 degrees
as he parts the customers' hair
takes the strain off his knees
and cuts a groove in the floor.

You pay as you leave
without supervision —
at 30 pence it must be
a snip for everyone.

But Sheffield's best short-cutter
soon will be gone:
after 40 years' service
the overheads have won.

To mark Attercliffe's lack
of its travelling barber
absence will surely make
the hair grow longer.

PAINTING THE LIGHT

Alfred Sisley, Moret-Sur-Loing, 1899

As I lie here
my retrospective
floats before my eyes:

a whole life-time's
struggles of completion,
yet no material progress!

I remember skies —
no mere background
but the source of action.

The clouds move across
like waves of the sea —
one is uplifted, carried along.

Sunlight softens
one part of the scene
and exalts another.

On Summer days
the wings on the blue —
what movement, such grace!

I have always believed
in showing the silver side,
but now I see

that when evening comes
clouds are thinning away
like distant furrows,

like eddies of water
frozen in air
upon which the sun sets —

I cannot combat any more —
very soon the night
will obscure my concerns.

I am going out
with the light I have painted
over and over.

GOODBYE MY LOVES

of Arshile Gorky (for Mimi)

His self he held at arm's length
inviting there plants, trees and grasses
to hold dialogue with him.
Eagerly they would push forward,
sway towards on long stalks,
bending like algae in the stream,
to meet and come amongst him.
So landscape became inscape
and Nature interpenetrated his dreams.

But how stand the uncertainty
of everything turned elemental? —
wind turns water turns molten,
the sun's stroke is a furnace,
dizziness overcomes his limbs,
his vision swims with the fronds,
consciousness dissolves away,
nothing stands between him and the flux —
GOODBYE MY LOVES. He is gone.

Now the paintings hang cool
in galleries where the long
pale fingers of light crawl
over whitewashed walls
towards them, and withdraw.

CHIAROSCURO

What it Was

It wasn't the heavenly Latin
cacophony of the Borghese dawn chorus

It wasn't the steaming capuccino odours
leaking from the Via Veneto's bars

It wasn't the feathering rainbows
of a score of Villa d'Este fountains

It was the small patch of sunlight
that crawls inside the roof of the Pantheon

In the Banca Di Santo Spirito

Glancing impassively over
his glasses over the heads of
those crowded around his desk:
pensioners, businessmen,
tourists, peasants from the hills —

he is a great leveller,
He holds their solvency
in his aloof stance. He brings
down the stamp THUMP
THUMP on their exposed lives.

At Perugia

Swifts are flying when they bury the old woman:
eighty years of labour lowered into the ground.
The alleluias of priest and mourners rise to the skies,
where swifts are cutting live air with their cries.

In Florence Station

Lowry would have loved

the old crone dressed in black
leaning on a luggage-trolley
around and around the concourse
as if amongst all those stopping-places
there was nowhere for her to go

back doubled over the handles
shoe-heels doubled over soles
the trolley bearing her along
face expressionless
pace funereal-slow

Easter Day

Bells ring out over the olive groves
on the foothills of the Gran Sasso.

An old man leans on his hoe and says
"In '43 I fought at Monte Cassino."

The cockerels call to each other
the name of this place: Contro-Guerra.

MONSOON

How capricious and spiteful you are
to keep me holding my breath
for that airy premonition!
Like a man in Trivandrum
I have begun to hallucinate:
for some, clouds sprout partridge feathers;
for some, sparrows mime in dustbowls;
and I — I have summoned the umbrellaman!

What propitiation may I make?
What enticement can I offer?
May my ragas not be accompanied
by the tabla but the tympanum
of the storm, so that when,

trailing glorious nets of fish,
and enabling lakes to sprout
green, you throw down
your annual unarguable challenge,
I shall follow your tumultuous
progress across a continent
till everything, even my thirst,
is quenched in Cherrapunji's torrents.

NOMADS

No miracles in the outback, but
mallee scrub — a sort of starker
silver birch, and many-trunked,
with rotten wood in every crevice —
occupies its arid acreages.

Also, of course, the budgerigars:
wild aboriginals of these lands,
their chirring chorussed warble
charting their nomadic ways
over the empty plains,
as here they settle in a leafstorm
beside some overflow bore,
or there onto a new nesting tree
(never the same place twice).

No miracles in the outback, but
bringing with them more than song,
the sudden spring blizzard alights,
and another barren mallee
is clothed in palpitating green.

IN NEBRASKA, DAKOTA, AND BEYOND ...

You will find them
down country roads with no name

fragile and forgotten
as nests the birds have abandoned

maybe no more now
than piles of collapsing clapboard

patches of honeysuckle paper
clinging to the walls

pink wainscotting, faded
recipes for fudge layer-cake

the empty rooms like pages
from a once-busy diary

you will stand there
eyes full of questions

without answers
before turning back

onto highways
obsessed with names

in Nebraska, Dakota
and beyond....

HARLEM AIRSHAFT

"The main thing, we can't get
a decent place to live
the rents so high
we have to go
where rents are cheap
to make a living
which keeps us low."

"Churches don't mean us
no good. We've been having
churches all our lives
under the same conditions
and look at the conditions
we're still in."

"I'm not a man,
none of us are men.
I don't own anything.
I'm not a man
enough to own a stone,
none of us are."

"I want to go to the veins."
"You want to do what?"
"I want to go to the veins."
"You mean you want to get high?"
"Yeah." "Why
do you want to get high, man?"
"To make me think."
"You can't think without getting high?"

"I don't think no
other people catch
as much hell as we do,
any place we go."

GOING TO MMBATHO

Going to Mmbatho
take the road from Jo'burg
that goes through Mafeking.
With that harmless, charm-
less dust-bowl of a dorp
have no trafficking
(though at least it exists
as a place to be besieged
and to be relieved).

"Going to Mmbatho?" —
the black man who stands
on the corner waves a hand:
"At the robot (traffic-light)
turn right. At the Total (garage)
turn left. And straight on
towards the horizon.
When you think you are
lost, then you are there."

Going to Mmbatho —
bare, monotonous, stark,
it stretches in an arc,
spare, uncultivated veld,
as far as there is,
a few thorn bushes,
thin covering of grass,
a land where even an ant-
hill is an event.

Going to Mmbatho —
how will you ever know
when you have arrived?

A scatter of chalets:
the Mmbatho Sun Hotel.
And rising from the plain
a tall scaffolding
in the shape of a stadium.
And that is all.

Nothing to detain you.
Just canned beer and music,
blackjack, roulette and lots
of fruit-machines. The Las
Vegas of the Fatherland!
And all of these amenities —
the food, drink, the pool,
Saturday-night dances —
are strictly for Afrikaners!

Coming from Mmbatho
there is no frontier
or border-post, no souvenir
(apart from 'Having Fun
at the Mmbatho Sun'
emblazoned on tee-
shirts), no brave
cheetah's head
on a little flag to wave.

Coming from Mmbatho
even those stands
will be dismantled,
were only after all
a portable skeleton
for carting off
and erecting again

a thousand miles away
at the next Independence Day.

Coming from Mmbatho
what will you remember
of the little you saw?
The unmade roads, mudhuts,
tumbledown stores, the dust,
the nakedness, the sores,
the squalor, poverty,
the crippled cars and lives:
a typical 'location',

Going to Mmbatho —
wasted journey, you say,
journey into a waste,
a place with just a name?
Yet this same Mmbatho
is where they must belong,
a nowhere to call home,
the capital of Bophuta
Tswana, their Bantustan!

UNDER THE WALL

At the Wall everything human stops.
Yesterday it was a man shot, trying
to escape from one world into another.

On both sides the tourists gather
to stand separately and gape.
Here taxis must turn; even the trams,
having reached no man's land, recoil
in search of some real-life destination.

But not quite everything human:
under it all a current flows
carrying the effluent of East to West.
While in the farms the sprinklers
purify without discrimination,
ceaselessly tracing their ritual circles.

THREE FROM INSIDE

ONE

Snuffling his way down corridors,
cocking a weather-snout for disasters,
it is of some rodent he reminds me.

He converses in a high-pitched whine
interspersed with grimaces and grunts —
even his statements are interrogatory:

"Is it bad, sir, is the weather bad
here, there, where, in Morecambe?
Will the snow fall?   Will it go on for ever?

Will the tide come over the sea-wall?
Will the wind blow and never stop?
That outside, sir, is it weather?"

Each day brings this whether-forecast,
my impossible meteorological quiz:
"Sir," (of an asterisk) "is that a snowflake?"

The movements of eyes and mind are merciless.
Whilst others doze and dream of release
"Come on, sir, tell me — you must stay awake!"

His one train journey ended in disaster:
"It was all the engine-driver's fault.
Instead of Preston I ended up in London —

he took the wrong track, then couldn't turn back!"
Yet in this place of so many outcasts
he is the harmless buffoon.

On his last night he dances on the table
and intones his mumbo-jumbo rhymes —
officers and his fellows roar their affection.

Tomorrow he'll be driven to Morecambe
where each tide will leave him gasping,
beached on the mudflats of rejection.

TWO

He wrote on every surface he could find:
doors, windows, walls, pavements, palings, railings ...

He employed every medium to hand:
pencils, pens, crayons, chalk, paint-brushes, spray-cans ...

And what did he write? Proper nouns, improper
names, salutations and denunciations

for someone or everyone or no-one
in a slanging mis-match of dialects.

When they caught up with him he was strapped and slapped,
bawled at and bawled out, fined and confined and bailed.

Finally, all his inarticulacies
were strung together to form one long sentence.

He was sent to a place surrounded by a
white fence on which he was forbidden to write.

So he pulled down the screen
in his mind and wrote on that.

THREE

This is the Nick that Jack burnt.
This is the Beast that lived in the Nick that Jack burnt.
This is the Con that got the Beast that lived
in the Nick that Jack burnt.
This is the Screw that beat the Con that got the Beast
that lived in the Nick that Jack burnt.
This is the Gov that told the Screw to beat the Con that got
the Beast that lived in the Nick that Jack burnt.

This is the Fuzz that caught the Jack that burnt the Nick.
This is the Beak that thanked the Fuzz for catching
the Jack that burnt the Nick.
This is the Nick where Jack was sent.
This is the Nick that Jack burnt.

HIT OR MISS

I was dumbfounded when he said
"Mr Zed, you're finished.
Get shut o' those tools.
Dae awa' wi' 'em."

I was staggered when he said
"Mr Zed, you're buggered.
You're to be fitted for a pacemaker."
It came very hard.

I was amazed when he said
"Is he dead, Mrs Zed?"
When they put the wires round my head
and sent me through the chamber.

I was scared when he said
"Are you Mr Zed?
I want to put the electrics on you."
It made my body gang altogether.

I'm starting to disfigure myself
through being out of sorts.
And the worst of all my troubles?
"It's hit or miss" he said.

IN THE DAY-CENTRE

Not here, where incongruous
heads and limbs abound,
eyes have it both ways,
twisted mouths emit sounds:

stuttering approximations
of their hearts' verities,
whilst others drool
helpless garrulities.

This is a book of parodies
or anthology of error:
handicap keeps them apart
yet brought them together;

the idea of perfection
exemplified by its lack,
a corrective of perspective —
God's self-study pack.

JANACEK

Tame as a dog,
rapacious as a vulture,
dry as a leaf,
lapping like the surf,
crackling like dry
twigs in the fire,
I cling to every
stirring of the mind,
numbed in
a holy silence.

*

Have you seen how a white flower
peels back the skin on a bud?
Have you ever heard a small
bird peck and peck
until he breaks his shell?
Have you lived through the storm
of streams of new ideas,
ones which tear and destroy?

*

The tame look
of a duckling, or
the scanning glance
of a hawk;
an ardent kiss
or the grasp
of a cooling hand;

the misty blue
of the forget-me-not,
or the burning fire
of the poppy:
all these create
in me a chord.

NUNS WITH CHAMBER ORCHESTRA

They had not heard the full consort before:
the way the wave gathers and spills,
taking its cue from and returning to stasis.

In the Interval they scamper among the music-stands:
"Here's the Viola — isn't its brown
tone like the stain on the refectory table!"

A day they are rehearsing for memory —
their animation defies annotation:
a pizzicato chatter, an aleatory chorus.

MOVEMENTS

1

Is this music walking very fast,
tripping, sprawling, getting to its feet,
increasing the beat,
stopping, starting, then running on?
I am getting very breathless
just listening. I can only just keep up.
I am very taken by the way it
manages to keep going,
the notes flowing,
but now slowing,
but I am glad when we at last
reach the first (and last) rest.

2

He finds a ball of wool
unwinds and unwinds;
he plays the Experience Game:
curls and uncurls and
pounces, rolls and whirls,
pretends uninterest, licks a paw,
then flicks out and in
and the chase is on as before.
Each time the ball unwinds
a little more until
once again he pounces ...
and there is nothing there.

3

It is raining
demi-semi-quavers in this landscape,
little downpours of notes —
I wish I had brought my umbrella.
Quick, quick, run for cover
into the next stave.

4

I am an ostinato,
I am searching for something
I cannot find, but
I keep on, it must be
around here somewhere,
I get the feeling
it is very near,
I keep turning back,
I must not stray
from the narrow track,
forgive me if I go
on repeating myself, but
I am an ostinato ...

5

Some days come running,
wagging their tails.
Other days drag into the light
some far-flung corpse.

Some days come marching,
waving their banners.
Other days plod, plod, plod
along the via dolorosa.

THE GOOSEBERRY GAME

You'll see us with our trouser-knees
all worn out, shoe-toes gone
with skrawking round looking at the gooseberries —
talk about funny positions! You'll see us
on our backs, on our knees,
on our sides, bottoms up in the air.
My wife says many a time
she wishes she'd got a gun
to have a pot at us.

You have to get the berries as big as
possible without bursting them.
The last week's the worst.
You keep them as dry as you can
and look at them about every two hours.
and if there's any sign of rain you cover them
to stop it getting to the roots.
You need a good woman
to look after them while you're at work.

You have every sort of pest to contend with.
I got moles very badly one year —
I caught thirteen in my gooseberry pen —
it was railroads-riddled about,
just like Crewe Station!

Flies are bad too. When a berry's dead ripe
if a fly only lands on it underneath
with the hairy suction of its feet
the weight of it can very nearly
draw the bottom out. You'll see the berry
go damp, and then it's not
long before it bursts.

Then there's wasps. You have to watch
and follow the wasp back to the nest.
A bloke told me
diesel was a good thing for wasps.
I put some on: it killed two trees.

We gather the berries the night before the show.
There has to be three gathering —
the one who grows the gooseberries,
and two others to see
that the berries aren't tied on, or anything like that.

They're gathered on plates, and then
they try to pick the heaviest and place them in a box.

These boxes have air-holes in them so that
the berries won't swell and burst. It's no use
if a gooseberry's bursted in the box

Some say fork in a barrowload of dead
rats in January. Some say give them
a little bit of waistcoat pocket.
There is no secret. You try all sorts.
You're a novice when you start, and
you're a novice when you finish, I reckon.

THE COMPOSER AND THE BIRDS

O to gather into one's memory
the rhythm of these coloured miracles —
from the yellow currant-leaves with silver edges
to the nebulous silver of the quiet river Visla
over which the crows flew away!

To remember too, in painful silence,
the gravelly, childish innocent voice
of a buzzard hung in a pool of cloud,
and to add to it the rhythm of agitated breathing
and the sad beat of a heart.

In whatever rhythm, whatever tempo
the crows wound into their brains
the beauty of these scenes
in the same rhythm they will unwind them
and the memories will call them home.

But what an uproar: as if clouds were colliding
the seven crows have already returned,
and their little sister hasn't finished her sewing —
how could she yet have collected
sufficient of the red sky of evening!

But whatever she has been able to catch
she throws over their shoulders.
Now how happily they shed their black feathers!
But one breathlessly tries in vain
to tear them from his right wing ...

Thus it is left to the composer
to inherit a black wing-tip,
who flies up and flourishes it,
his creative gift, high in the sky —
though careful to keep one foot on the ground!

IN THE GARDEN

(for Myra)

There is always a child in the garden.

At first it is oneself:
who mounts expeditions into
the frightful jungle shrubbery
in search of the magic bush
that towers in the clearing
its humming intoxicant powers
protected by a ring of stings.

Then the child is one's own:
a threat to the precarious order
you have finicked into existence
in rows and precise irregularities,
black, weedless earth poised for
the footprint of the explorer —
irritant, cause for quickened pulse-rate.

Later the child in the garden may be
almost the last thing that you see:
a delicately poised particularity
framed by cypress-hedge and apple-tree
but growing smaller all the while
as in an old master miniature
hung in the long gallery of memory.

GARDEN OF LOVE

And now I am enclosed
by high walls; enter this
secret midwinter world's
sempiternal stasis:

underfoot sodden leaves,
raw sticks, lie where they fell.
I pass through greenhouses
neglected, cold, the paint
peeling, some of the panes
shattered, pipes furred with rust.

Then I see it: startling
crimson camellia —
its petals firm-folded,
illumining the gloom.
Parting the leaves I find
that the bloom bears her name.

DREAM-SEQUENCE

1

She talks to me of
the day she lay
on a mountain
and a hand descended.

She talks to me of
the night a red man
with horns and pitchfork
forced her to eat stones.

She talks to me of
her skin coming off
and floating away
but the bones remain.

She talks to me of
scaling a lamppost
to reach the sky
and jumping upwards.

2

Her impassivity to my imploring
is like the infliction of internal wounds
by a sword that never leaves its sheathe.
Or her welcoming and its aftermath
is like a dream I have of endless
corridors down which I travel
and at each turning her dear
face beckons till at last
I catch up with a slap in the face.

3

In the pit of the heart
it grips you and won't let go:
a little grey furry creature
that comes in out of the snow

surrounding us; it sidles,
nosing for an entrance,
and it has fetching ways,
insinuations to entrance

the most inhospitable.
You give it licence to roam
your innermost secrets.
It curls up in its new home

secure in your confidences
as if it has earned them.
Suddenly you realise
how vulnerable you have become.

It attacks by default —
small acts of carelessness
cause the most distress.
It cannot be cast out.

In the pit of the heart
it grips you and won't let go ...

NIGHT TRAIN

Night train roars, punches a hole in the dark.

And every terror is unleashed to run wild
down the corridors — fleeting forms in doorways;
frightful family secrets on racks and under seats;
faces in mirrors over the washbasins
making grimaces that are your own;
screwed into a carriage-corner each blare
of the diesel's klaxon signifies despair ...

Till day disperses, marking at least a truce —
in a shell-burst of light, a scatter of hope,
hillsides reassemble, horizons reinstate,
streets are rinsed clear; as the brakes begin to bite
you feel a strange lightening of the burden you carry;
there is time to uncrumple, smoothe down your soul,
before stepping out soberly to meet the day.

While Night train to wait in a siding is shunted away.

THE SNOWMAN

Crossing the border
into blizzard country,
the plough upfront
spuming furrows
fails — helplessly we
nosedive the pillows.

Sudden silence
between and around us;
sudden stillness —
a calm descends
upon those who know
they can go no further.

I step out into
unfenced existence,
hold arms wide,
feeling flakes glide,
settle upon my palms,
begin their disguise.

DIVINING

More than a decade since we met:

not surprising your scalp has shed
its camouflage, and the tendons
of your neck strain threateningly.

Yet the adrenalin runs free:
you have taken up dowsing, and
want to share this accomplishment.

I hold the coat-hanger stalks out
straight, take a slow-motion walk, then
suddenly they tweak till they cross.

It is all out of our control.

TRIPTYCH

1

I remember rows with him when
the mouth would open and close
and open, and the sounds that emerged
were those of petulant reproach,
an infantile thwarting of will.

Sound and fury dissolved away,
now he is seen as he always was:
a fish out of his element
blowing empty bubbles into air
signifying sheer helplessness.

2

How a house takes on
the temperament of its owner:
always before, this bungalow
was a repository of temper,
like a coiled spring ready
at any time to unclinch
and spreadeagle all persons
unwise enough to enter.

Now, lacking his charge,
it seems feeble, slack,
free of impediment
for the first time —
perhaps we might even
begin to impose our own
personas, before it
passes out of patrimony.

3

What made her wake —
was it the obscene mockery of the seagulls,
the foghorn blurting over the sandbank?

What made her wake —
was it the memory of his calls in the night,
the stark constrictions of his fight for breath?

What made her wake
was the clock picking over the bones of the hours,
the empty endless aftermath of death.

LOSING WIN

Hers is a clown's face,
pasty complexion
with a puckering lip

and two black button eyes.
When she grins
it swallows the gloom

of her surroundings:
a caring-place
for the almost-gone.

Her jokey view:
looking from the window
onto a building-site:

"Who'd have thought
I'd end my days
getting worked up
over dumper-trucks
zooming about!"

*

Now, six months on,
she can't turn her head,
wincing even to smile.

Motorised at last,
she lacks motivation
to go anywhere again.

And her voice, wavering
faintly, as if beamed
from somewhere beyond.

Driving home through the dark
and rain, I question
the reason for pain.

Only the relentless swipe-
swipe of the wipers
keeps me on the road.

HOSPICE VOICES

1

We don't like holding them,
those exposed parts trailing from our arms.

We don't like them being grasped,
those tell-tale sweaty members.

But here it doesn't worry me.
It's the pressure that reassures.

I have done it for others,
what I could not do for my husband.

2

Coming second all the time —
that's the story of my life.

Then I got sick: and here I am
getting pampered all the time.

I've never known such treatment.
But when I look round the ward

I just can't help wondering
who's going to go second.

3

We told him we loved him
and he crinkled an eyelid
and a little tear ran down.

You get ready for death,
but you're not prepared,
you can't really comprehend.

He went with great dignity,
and I've promised him
the rest will be up to his standard.

LAST PHOTOGRAPH OF THE MOTHER-IN-LAW

She tilts out of the frame
towards us, a half-smile
teetering on her lips:

widow on holiday
enjoying brief Indian Summer
before the cold sets in.

How fortuitous
she is caught at the height
of the swing's momentum:

out of the valley
of the shadow of husband
into the sunlit
meadow of her self.

AFTER-IMAGE

What would I preserve of me?
Today it is the ripe Autumnal smell
of woodsmoke as night approaches:

an expiring exhalation, burning,
but slow, without intensity,
pungent, and wholly impersonal.

LINES ON LINES

My love left his first lines
behind the loosened stones.

I would go from place to place
to complete each couplet.

Now that my love is gone
I seek out those buildings

but find them in ruins.
I turn over the stones:

this search for beginnings,
can it have any end?